Circus Performers

Diana Noonan

Contents

Circus Performers

The Circus and Its Performers

A circus is a group of strong, athletic performers who use their special skills to amaze and entertain people.

Some circuses travel from place to place and perform in large tents. Other circuses stay in one place and perform in halls and theatres.

Each time it arrives at a new place, this circus sets up a tent.

Circus performers are trained in one, or more, of the four main types of circus skills. These skills are juggling, balancing, **acrobatics** and performing magic tricks. Circus performers often go to special classes to help them learn these skills.

Circus performers need to be very fit to do their jobs.

This performer is part of a circus that performs on a theatre stage.

Magicians

Circus magicians amaze their audiences with magic tricks. They use special equipment when they perform, including hats, scarves, cards and magic wands.

A magician can pick out the card you chose without having seen it before!

Some circus magicians invite people from the audience to help them with their tricks during a performance.

A person may be given a magic wand to hold, only to find that the wand becomes floppy!

Or they may be invited to pull a single silk scarf from a hat, then find the scarf has become joined onto a long line of other scarves, as if by magic.

A magician pretends to pull a scarf out of a boy's sleeve.

Jugglers

Juggling is the skill of keeping three or more objects moving through the air without dropping them.

There are two main types of juggling: toss and bounce.

In toss juggling, the juggler tosses several objects up into the air before catching them. They do this again and again.

In bounce juggling, the juggler bounces several unbreakable objects off a hard surface and catches them over and over.

toss juggling with rings

bounce juggling with balls

Jugglers often include other circus skills in their acts. They may ride a unicycle or walk along a low **cable** as they juggle.

A juggler uses different parts of their body to toss, bounce and catch. They may toss a plate into the air with their foot, and catch it on their back, or bounce a ball off their knee and catch it under their chin.

Juggling while riding a unicycle makes the trick more difficult.

Balance Performers

Some circus performers are skilled at balancing. To perform their acts, they must be fit, daring and have good concentration.

It is important for them to eat healthy food and to exercise often so that their muscles stay strong.

Many balancing acts take place on the ground, but some of the most exciting acts are performed high up on narrow wires.

These skilled performers need to be careful not to unbalance each other.

The stilts make the performers much taller than everyone else.

Some circus performers balance on stilts. Stilts are poles made of metal or wood. They have footrests part-way up for the performer to stand on. Straps hold the stilts to the performer's legs. When long stilts are hidden by clothing, the performer appears to be very tall.

Some performers balance on a roller board. A roller board is a short board placed on top of a metal cylinder. A performer can do handstands on their roller board, or balance on a board placed on a whole stack of cylinders.

This roller-board performer has to stay balanced while moving.

Balance performers know how to walk on giant balls called "walking globes". A beginner globe-walker may train on a globe filled with sand. The sand makes the globe heavy, and easier to balance on. When the performer gets better at balancing, they walk on a globe without any sand inside it.

Many globe-walkers can perform other circus skills, such as juggling, as they walk on the globe.

Bicycles and unicycles are used in balancing acts in different ways. Sometimes, several performers balance on one bike or unicycle as one person pedals.

There are ten performers on this bike!

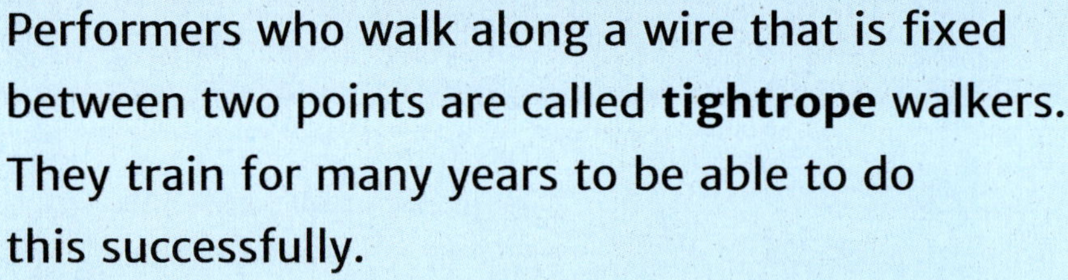

Performers who walk along a wire that is fixed between two points are called **tightrope** walkers. They train for many years to be able to do this successfully.

Tightrope walkers use both low and high wires. Low wires are around 2 metres off the ground. High wires are at least 4.5 metres off the ground.

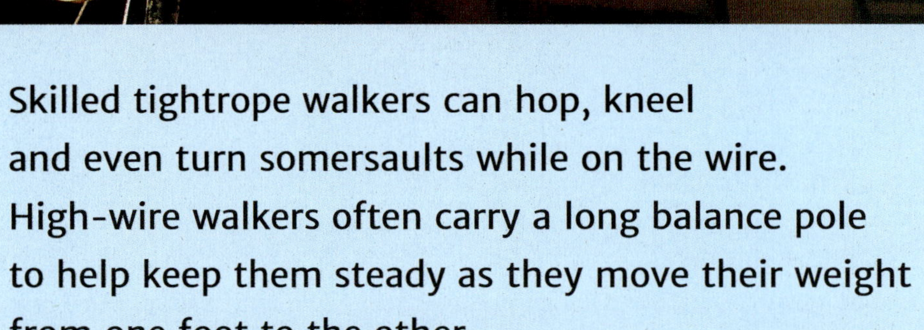

Skilled tightrope walkers can hop, kneel and even turn somersaults while on the wire. High-wire walkers often carry a long balance pole to help keep them steady as they move their weight from one foot to the other.

Two tightrope walkers walk across a high wire while balancing a third performer.

Acrobats

Acrobatic acts combine circus and gymnastic skills, and are performed on the ground or in the air. An acrobat requires strength, balance and perfect timing to perform their acts.

Acrobats performing in the air use special **harnesses** which allow them to spin, twist and cartwheel without becoming tangled in the safety line that holds them.

A harness is needed to perform acrobatic acts in the air.

Acrobats use equipment such as hoops and ladders. Hoop acrobats use a combination of gymnastic moves and dance moves to entertain their audience.

Safety equipment is important, especially when acrobats are performing high in the air.

Acrobats often use several circus skills at once. They may climb and balance their way up a ladder, then juggle when they reach the top.

These performers are doing acrobatics on a ladder.

Many acrobats use no equipment at all.
They rely on their strong muscles and fit bodies
to somersault, leap and tumble.
They are skilled at working with other acrobats
to balance, and to create arches, towers and pyramids
with their bodies.

Acrobats create a four-level pyramid by arching their bodies.

Aerial Performers

Acrobats who perform in the air are called **aerial** acrobats. They show off their difficult gymnastic moves high above the ground. Their acts are often the most exciting part of a circus.

Aerial acrobats are usually attached to safety lines. A safety line is used to raise or lower the performer.

Aerial acrobats use equipment such as silks and straps. Silks are pieces of strong fabric which the performer can hang from, sit in, or use as a hammock in the air.

Straps are very strong belts that hang from above. Aerial acrobats use these belts like gymnasts use bars.

Straps performers need a lot of upper body strength.

One of the best-known pieces of circus equipment is the trapeze. A trapeze is a short bar hung on cables high above the audience. There are two styles of trapeze: fixed and flying.

These performers are using a fixed trapeze.

Performers on a fixed trapeze carry out their acrobatic moves while the trapeze stays mainly in one place.

Flying trapeze performers carry out their moves while the trapeze is swinging. These acts often involve one performer swinging off the bar and being caught, mid-air, by another performer.

One performer has swung off the flying trapeze, ready to be caught by the second performer.

As long as circus performers continue to amaze audiences and make them laugh, circuses will always be enjoyed as a special kind of entertainment.

How to Perform a Magic Wand Trick

Learning circus skills can help improve your fitness and concentration. Circus skills such as roller-board balancing and magic tricks are sometimes taught in schools.

This magic wand trick is fun to perform for others. You will need to practise the steps many times in front of a mirror before you perform the trick to an audience.

Goal

To perform a magic wand trick

Materials

- a mirror
- a small table
- a magician's wand (or a chopstick)

Steps

1. Stand in front of the mirror and turn side-on. Imagine that the mirror is your audience. Place the wand on the table in front of you.

2. Hold out your left arm so that the back of your left hand is facing the mirror.

3. Grip your left wrist with your right hand. As you do, keep your right index finger against your left palm.

4. Still gripping your left wrist, pick up the wand from the table with your left hand. Hold it up and practise saying: "This wand is magic. It can stick to the palm of my hand."
5. Tuck the wand under your left thumb and right index finger. Hold the wand firmly against your left palm.

6. Stretch out the fingers on your left hand. Hold up your left thumb and wiggle it. Practise saying: "See how the wand sticks to my hand?"

7. Practise saying: "Now, watch as I stop the wand from sticking to the palm of my hand." After saying this, blow on the wand. As you blow, release your right index finger so that the wand falls to the ground.

8. When you have practised the trick and you are feeling confident, it is time to perform it for an audience. Your audience will think that you really can make the wand stick to your hand by magic and release it again by blowing on it!

Glossary

acrobatics (*noun*) displays of gymnastic moves and skills on the ground or in the air

aerial (*adjective*) happening in the air

cable (*noun*) a thick rope or wire that is really strong

harnesses (*noun*) special straps that support someone's body

tightrope (*noun*) a rope or wire stretched tightly between two points above the ground

Index